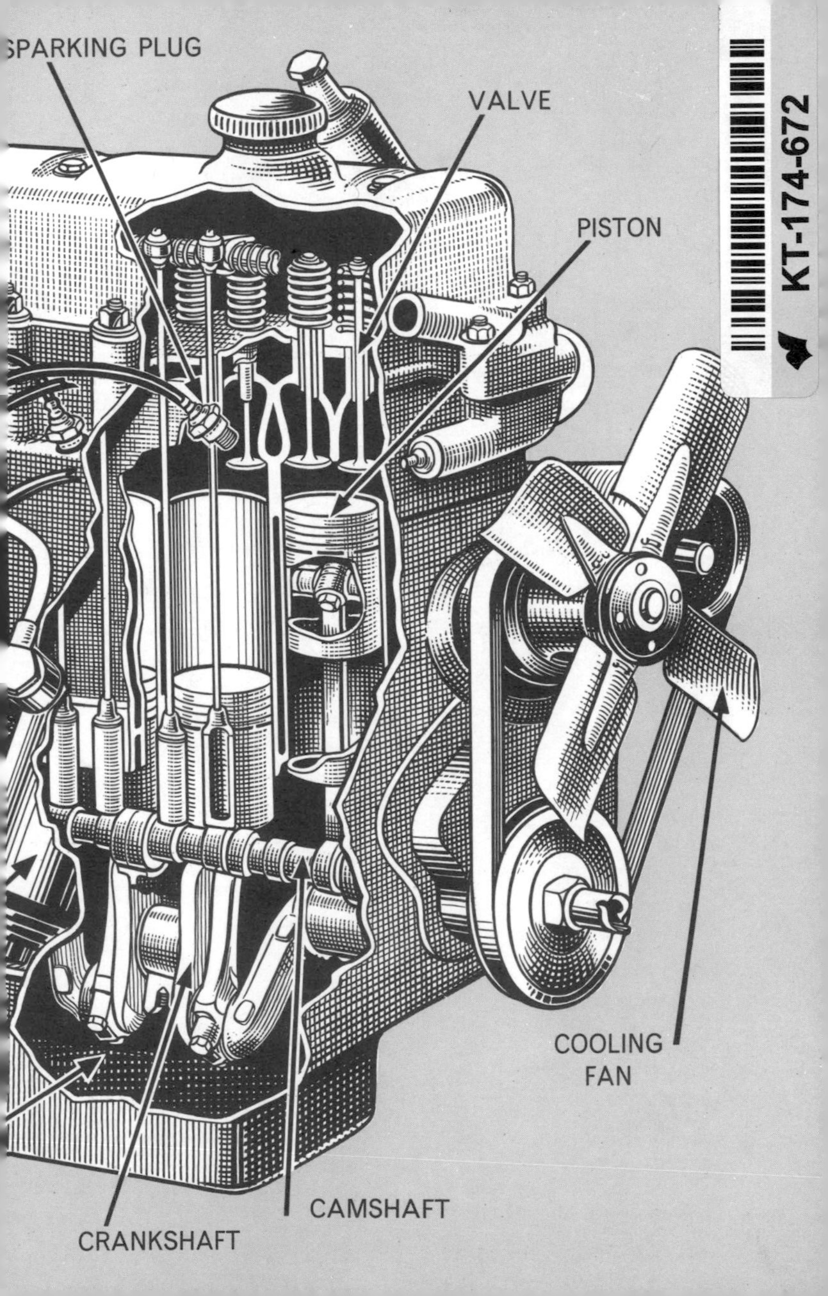
SPARKING PLUG
VALVE
PISTON
COOLING FAN
CAMSHAFT
CRANKSHAFT

Series 654

*Here is a book which all boys will find fascinating, and which will be equally interesting and instructive to many adults—particularly those learning to drive.*

*With the aid of excellent colour illustrations and diagrams it explains simply and clearly the different parts and working units of a car, and their position and function in the general design.*

A
LADYBIRD
BOOK

2/6
NET

# How it works:

# THE MOTOR CAR

*by*

DAVID CAREY

Publishers: Wills & Hepworth Ltd., Loughborough

*First published 1965*  *Printed in England*

## *How it works: The MOTOR CAR*

The motor car is a form of mechanical transport and it is composed of many different working units and parts. To provide the energy to make it go, it has an engine which in turn needs electric current, petrol and air. The engine needs cooling so that it does not become too hot, and oil to lubricate the bearing surfaces.

Also, there is the transmission system of clutch, gearbox, propeller shaft and axle, which transmits the power from the engine to the wheels to move the car along the road. Steering mechanism is needed to guide the car in the right direction, brakes to slow it down and stop it, and suspension to smooth out most of the bumps and jolts.

A sectioned view of a typical car is shown on the opposite page and from this you can see how some of the major units fit into the general design. In the pages that follow we will examine each unit in turn and find out how it does its job. The engine is the most complicated unit, and several pages are used to describe simply and clearly the various operations and systems that combine to make it work.

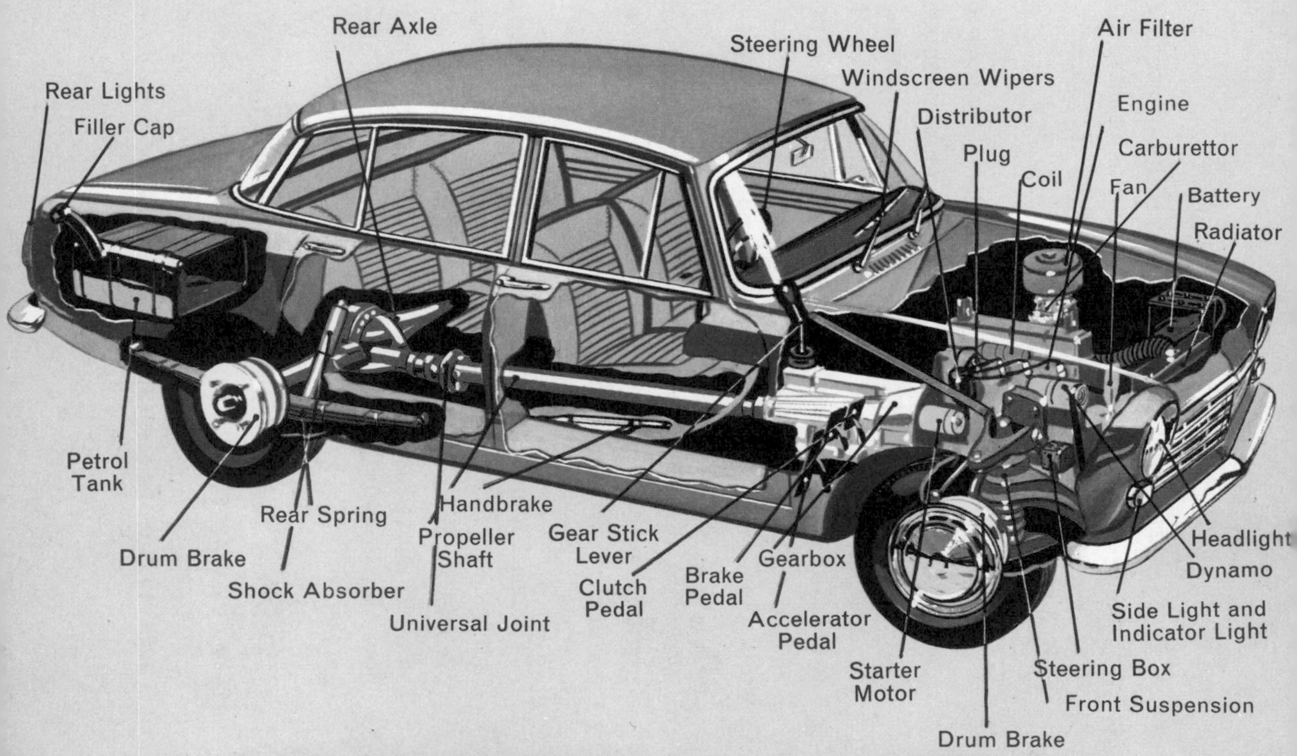
Rear Axle
Steering Wheel
Air Filter
Windscreen Wipers
Rear Lights
Filler Cap
Engine
Distributor
Carburettor
Plug
Coil
Fan
Battery
Radiator
Petrol Tank
Handbrake
Rear Spring
Gear Stick Lever
Propeller Shaft
Drum Brake
Brake Pedal
Gearbox
Clutch Pedal
Shock Absorber
Universal Joint
Accelerator Pedal
Headlight
Dynamo
Side Light and Indicator Light
Starter Motor
Steering Box
Front Suspension
Drum Brake

## *The Electrical System*

Every petrol-engined car needs electricity to provide current for the lights and other electrical equipment, and to supply the necessary power for the ignition system.

The *ignition system* enables the engine to be started and kept running, and sparking plugs form an essential part of this system. They are screwed into the engine at, or near, the top, usually one sparking plug for each cylinder. A four-cylinder engine therefore has four sparking plugs, a six-cylinder engine six sparking plugs, and so on. As the name suggests, the purpose of a sparking plug is to make a spark, and this spark is achieved by making the electric current jump a gap between two points (known as 'electrodes') which are at the extreme end of the plug which is inserted in the cylinder.

The spark ignites the fuel/air mixture in each cylinder, and very rapid burning and expansion results. This process is called 'combustion' and it takes place in the 'combustion chamber'. It will be explained later just how this combustion fits into the operation of the engine.

Electricity for the igniting process (ignition) is supplied by a dynamo and battery (*page 8*). The current is then carried to a coil (*page 10*), then to a distributor (*page 12*) and finally to the sparking plugs.

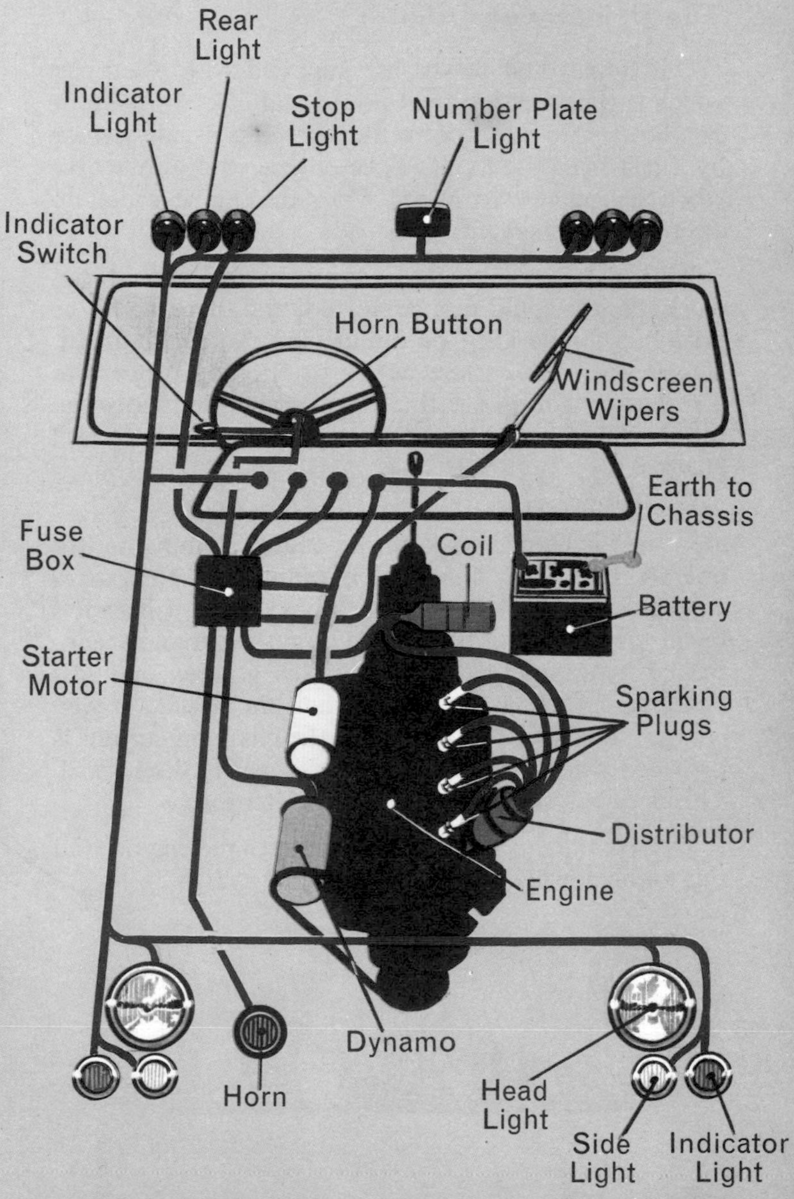

Rear Light
Indicator Light
Stop Light
Number Plate Light
Indicator Switch
Horn Button
Windscreen Wipers
Earth to Chassis
Fuse Box
Coil
Battery
Starter Motor
Sparking Plugs
Distributor
Engine
Dynamo
Horn
Head Light
Side Light
Indicator Light

## *The Dynamo and Battery*

Our homes and towns are supplied with electricity which is generated in great power stations. In a motor car the *dynamo* is the power station. It is usually driven by a belt from the front of the engine, and only works when the engine is running. When the engine is idle, no electricity is generated.

Without electricity the ignition system would not work, the car could not be started, and there would be no lights for parking or for driving the car at night. This is where the *battery* does a useful job. It provides a means of storing electricity which can be used when the dynamo is not operating, and it must be kept well charged.

Under normal circumstances more current is generated than is needed to keep the engine running and to operate the other electrical equipment. This extra current is used to charge the battery so that it will always be in good condition. The charging current is controlled by a voltage regulator: this ensures that less charging current is generated when the battery is well charged, and that an increase in the charging current is provided when the battery becomes partly discharged. This is called 'compensated voltage control'.

The dynamo and starter are bolted to the engine, and this automatically 'earths' them to the chassis.

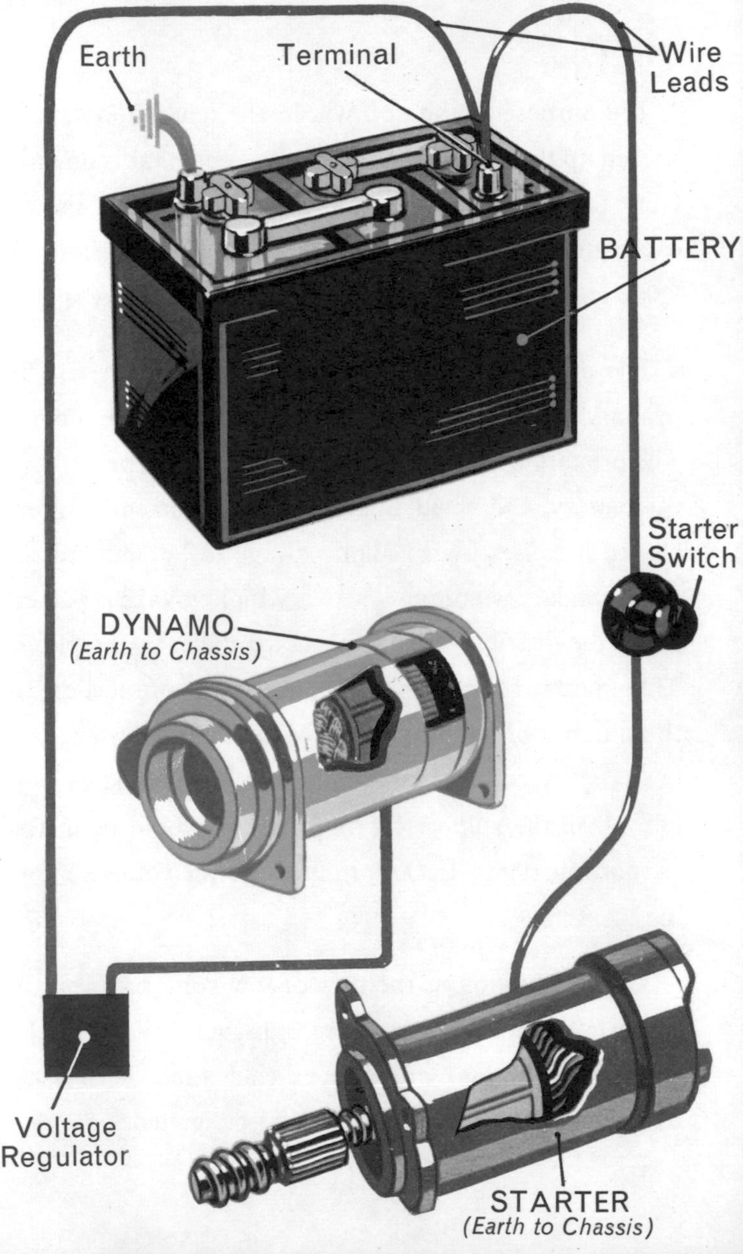
Earth
Terminal
Wire Leads
BATTERY
Starter Switch
DYNAMO
(Earth to Chassis)
Voltage Regulator
STARTER
(Earth to Chassis)

### *The Coil*

The purpose of the *coil* within the ignition system is to step up the electrical pressure (*voltage*) that is flowing from the battery to the sparking plugs. Most motor car batteries are of the 12 volt type, but as many as 7,000 volts may be required to give a satisfactory spark.

The coil actually consists of two coils of wire, the primary and the secondary, wound round an iron core. The primary coil is fed with low voltage electricity from the battery, and when this low voltage current is interrupted it causes a very high voltage to be 'induced' in the secondary winding. This very high voltage is passed on to the distributor and thence to the sparking plugs. The amount of increase in voltage is in proportion to the number of windings in each coil. For instance, if the primary coil has 100 winds and the secondary coil has 1,000, the voltage leaving the coil would be in the proportion 100 to 1,000, or ten times the voltage entering it.

The interruption in the flow of low voltage current in the primary winding (causing a higher voltage in the secondary winding) must occur each time the fuel/air mixture in any cylinder is ready to be ignited.

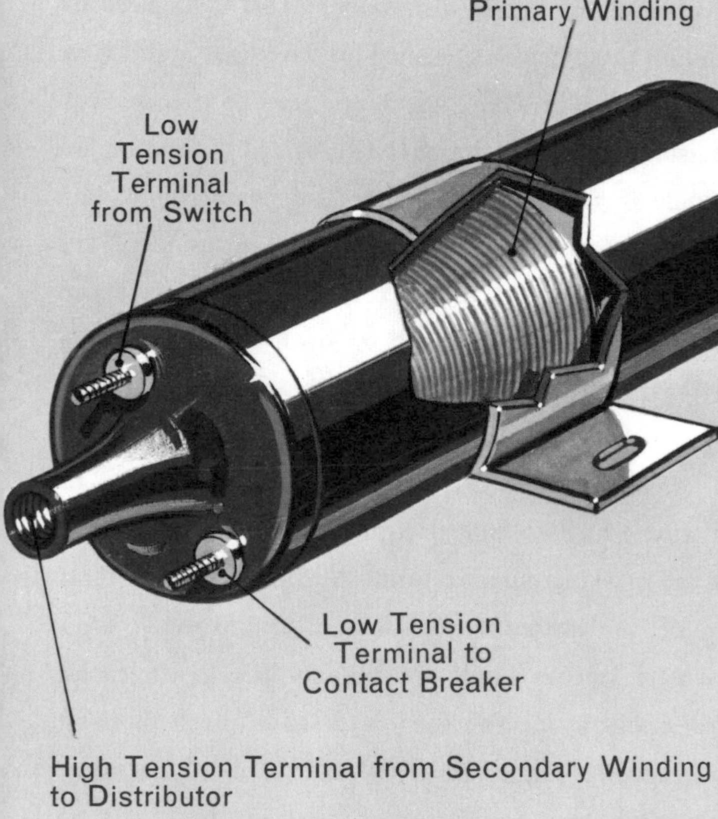
Primary Winding
Low Tension Terminal from Switch
Low Tension Terminal to Contact Breaker
High Tension Terminal from Secondary Winding to Distributor

### *The Distributor*

Interruption of the low voltage flow to the coil, referred to on the preceding page, is made by contact breaker points in the *distributor*. This final piece of ignition equipment is mounted on the engine and driven by a spindle, or shaft, which connects to a gear on a camshaft inside the engine (*page 20*). At the top of the spindle is a cam which, instead of being round, has 'corners', there being as many 'corners' as there are sparking plugs. As the cam rotates, the 'corners' cause the contact breaker points to open and close, thus giving the off-on effect needed by the coil.

The distributor also has another function, that is to distribute high-voltage electricity from the coil to each of the sparking plugs in turn. A rotor arm is fitted on top of the distributor cam. The rotor arm rotates with the cam, and in doing so contacts in turn the metal projections inside the distributor cap. Each of these projections is connected to a sparking plug so that when the rotor arm contacts a projection, high voltage electricity is passed to the plug concerned and a spark occurs at the electrodes.

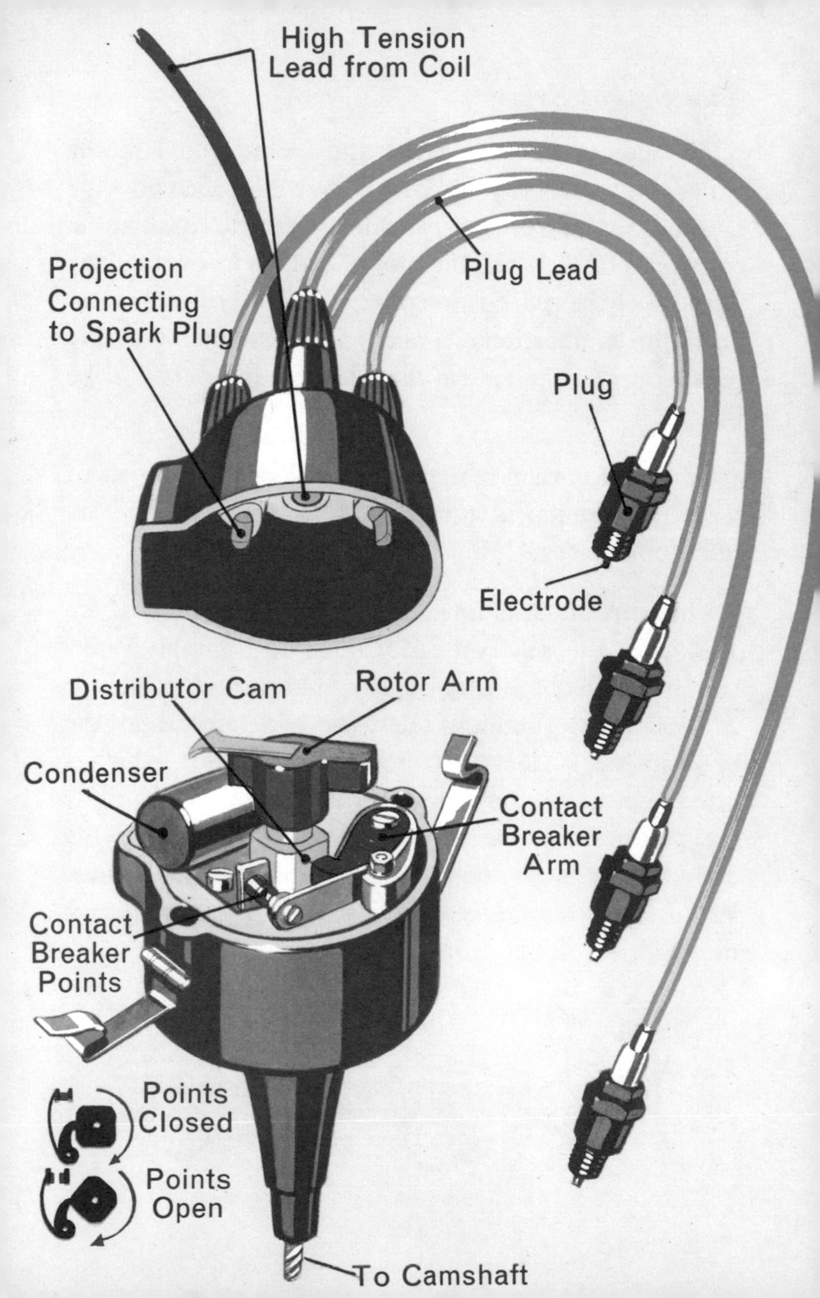
High Tension Lead from Coil
Projection Connecting to Spark Plug
Plug Lead
Plug
Electrode
Distributor Cam
Rotor Arm
Condenser
Contact Breaker Arm
Contact Breaker Points
Points Closed
Points Open
To Camshaft

## *The Petrol System*

Two elements are needed for the operation of a motor car engine: electricity and petrol. We have seen how the ignition system works to provide an electric spark at the electrodes of the sparking plugs, and we know that the purpose of the spark is to ignite a mixture of petrol and air in the combustion chambers of the engine. Now we must consider the system that delivers the petrol to be ignited.

In cars of normal design, the *petrol system* consists of three main units: a storage tank, a pump and a carburettor (*see page 16*).

The petrol tank is fitted at the back of the car where it is out of the way, yet easily filled at a garage. Tanks vary in capacity but they usually hold enough petrol for 250-300 miles running. Because the tank is at the opposite end of the car from the carburettor, which is fitted high up on the engine, a pump is needed to draw the petrol from one to the other, as it is from the carburettor that the petrol is finally fed into the engine. Pumps can be of two kinds; electrically operated or mechanically driven from the engine.

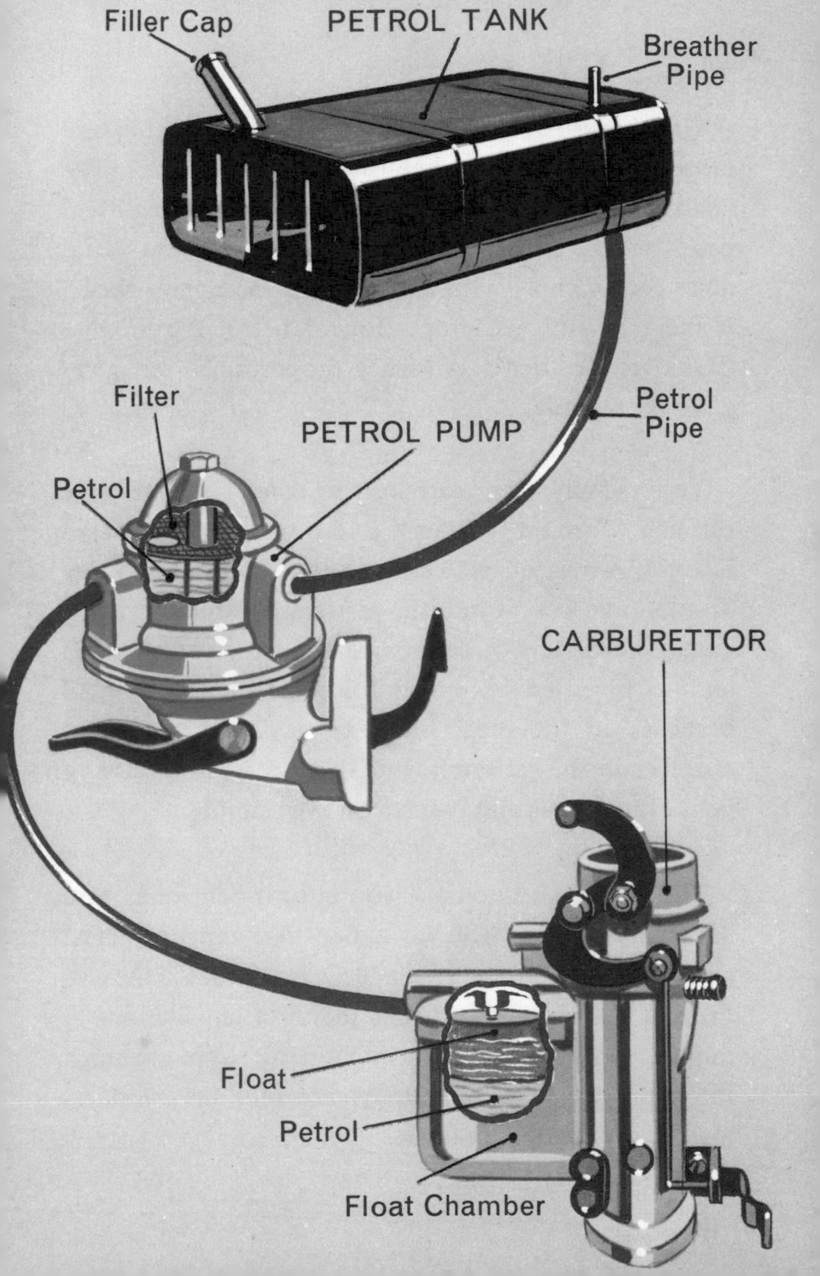
Filler Cap
PETROL TANK
Breather Pipe
Petrol Pipe
Filter
PETROL PUMP
Petrol
CARBURETTOR
Float
Petrol
Float Chamber

### *The Carburettor*

The purpose of the *carburettor* is to provide a mixture of petrol and air for combustion in the engine. The mixture normally consists of one part (by weight) of petrol to fifteen parts of air, but this mixture varies quite considerably with temperature and engine speed. If there is a higher proportion of petrol the mixture is said to be 'rich'. A higher proportion of air gives a 'weak' mixture.

Very simply, the carburettor consists of a tube through which air is drawn, and a series of very small holes known as jets which break the petrol up into tiny droplets and pass it into the airstream in the form of a mist. The mixture of petrol mist and air is sucked along an inlet pipe (induction manifold) and then, by way of branches in the pipe, into each cylinder. A float chamber in the carburettor provides a small reserve of petrol for the jets and ensures an even supply.

The flow of air into the carburettor is controlled by a 'butterfly throttle', which is a flap that can be opened and closed by operating the accelerator pedal in the car. Pressing the accelerator opens the throttle. This lets in more air which in turn sucks more petrol vapour through the main jet. The mixture passes into the cylinders making the engine run faster.

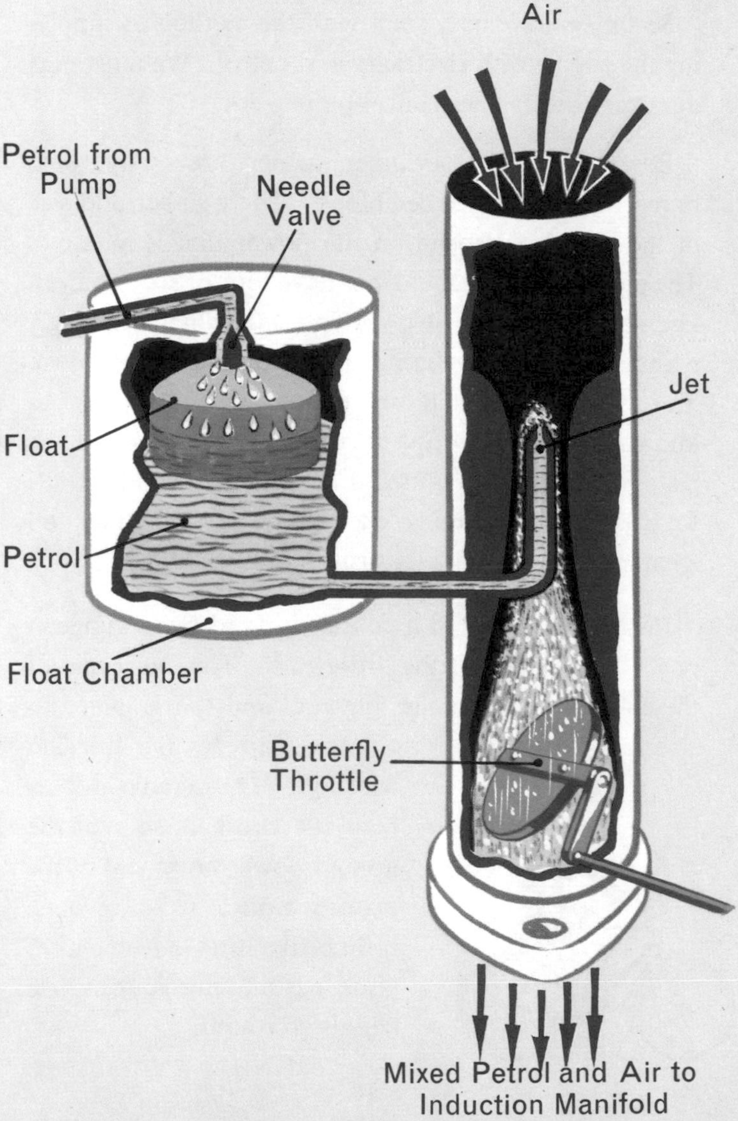
Air
Petrol from
Pump
Needle
Valve
Jet
Float
Petrol
Float Chamber
Butterfly
Throttle
Mixed Petrol and Air to
Induction Manifold

## *The Pistons and Crankshaft*

So far we have only dealt with the method of supplying the engine with electricity and petrol. We must next discover how the mechanical parts work.

Every engine has cylinders which are really tubes bored out of the cylinder block. The number and size of the cylinders depend on the power that is required. The most common car engines have four or six cylinders. Each cylinder is provided with a *piston* which fits snugly within the cylinder walls but is able to slide up and down. The movement of a piston up or down a cylinder is known as a stroke. Spring rings are fitted round the pistons. They press outward against the cylinder walls to prevent air escaping downward or too much oil escaping upward between piston and cylinder.

Pistons are joined to a connecting rod by a 'gudgeon pin'. This joint is at the 'little-end'. The lower end of the connecting rod is the 'big-end' and this is joined to a *crankshaft* by the 'big-end bearing'. The crankshaft is bent, or cranked, so that the up and down movement of the pistons causes it to revolve, rather like the movement of your legs making your bicycle pedals go round.

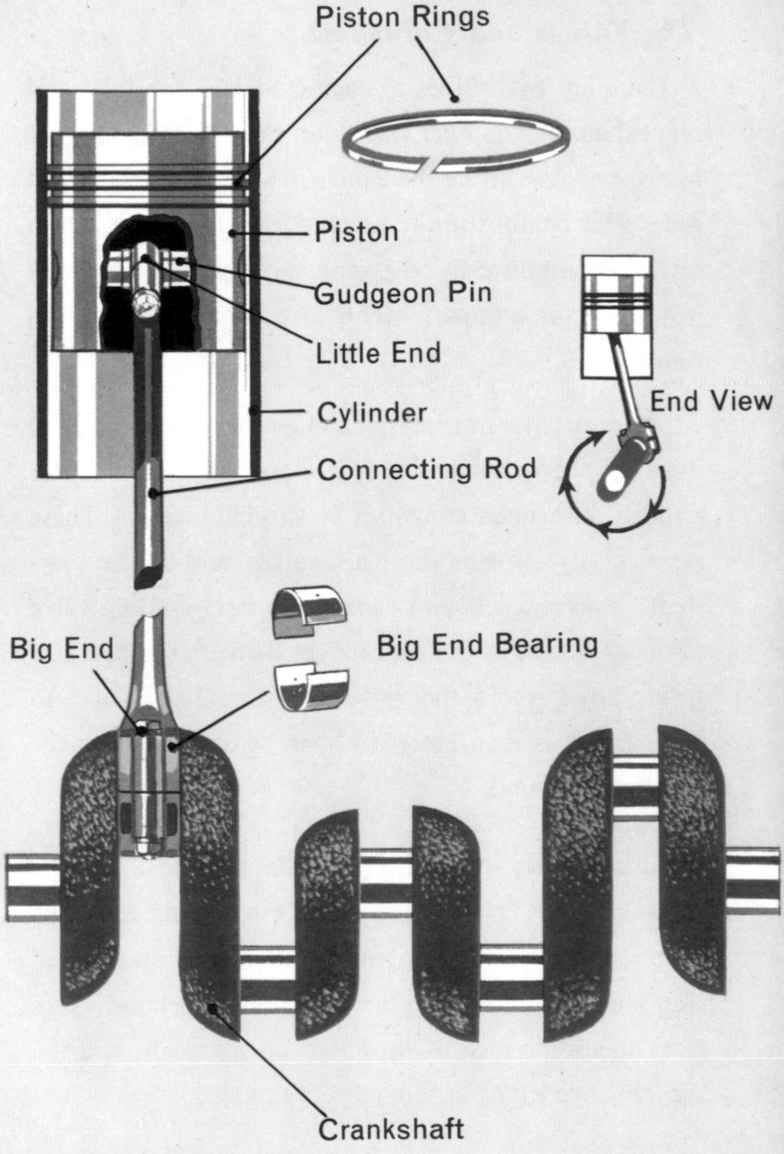
Piston Rings
Piston
Gudgeon Pin
Little End
Cylinder
Connecting Rod
End View
Big End
Big End Bearing
Crankshaft

### *The Valves and Camshaft*

There are two valves to each cylinder: one inlet and one exhaust. The *inlet valves* let the petrol/air mixture into the engine, while the *exhaust valves* allow the burnt gases after combustion to escape from the engine. Both sets of valves have to be arranged to open and close at just the right moment. This is done by means of a *camshaft*.

The camshaft is driven by a chain or gear at half the speed of the crankshaft. It has specially-shaped projections, known as cams, set at varying angles. There are as many cams as there are valves, and as the camshaft revolves, each cam causes its corresponding valve to open. Then, as the cam moves further round, a coil spring fitted round the valve stem forces the valve to shut, and it is then ready to open again next time the cam comes round.

During every revolution of the camshaft all the valves open and close once. In a fast-moving car fitted with a four-cylinder engine, each valve opens and closes between thirty and forty times every second. This gives you some idea of the speed of operation and the accuracy needed to obtain correct timing.

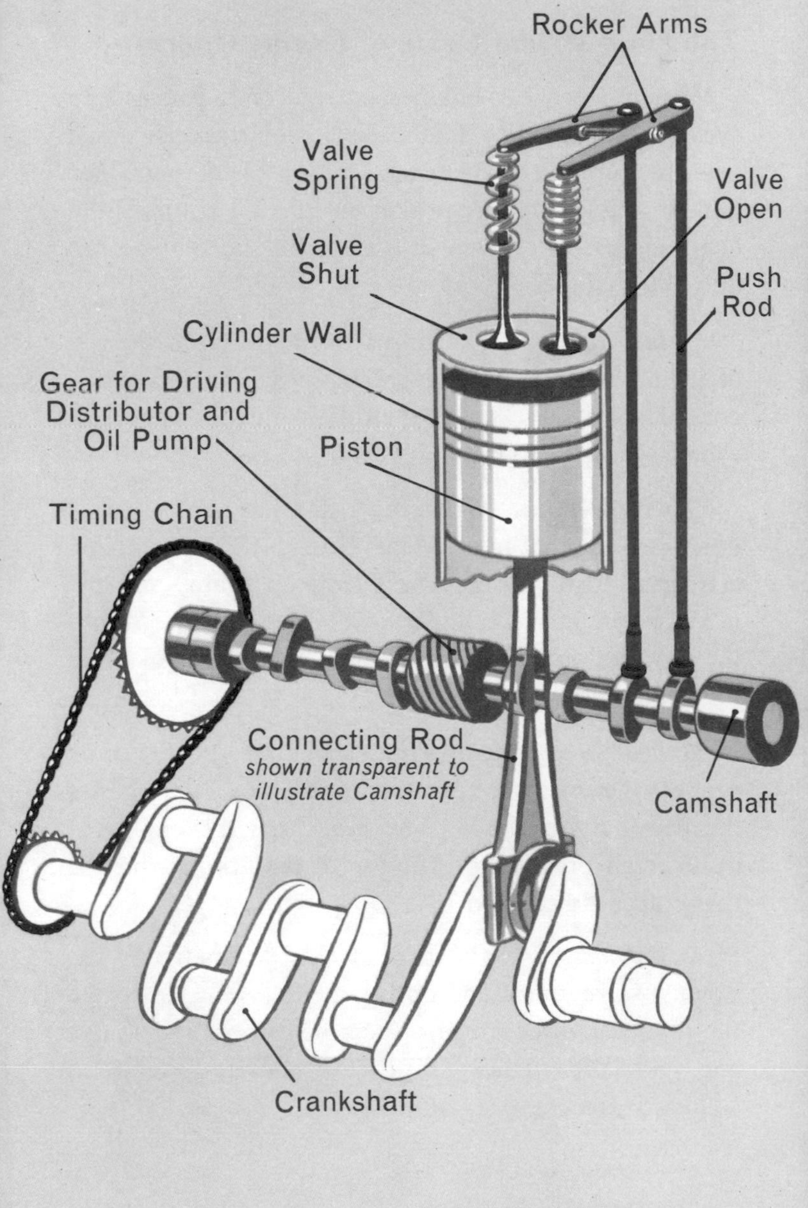
Rocker Arms
Valve
Spring
Valve
Open
Valve
Shut
Push
Rod
Cylinder Wall
Gear for Driving
Distributor and
Oil Pump
Piston
Timing Chain
Connecting Rod
shown transparent to
illustrate Camshaft
Camshaft
Crankshaft

## *The Four-stroke Cycle of Engine Operation*

Most modern car engines operate on a four-stroke cycle. This means that each piston travels down twice and up twice after each ignition of the petrol/air mixture, making four strokes in all. To simplify the operating sequence, we will assume that our engine has only one cylinder.

(1) *Induction.* This begins with the piston at the top of its stroke and the inlet valve open. As the piston goes down it draws the petrol/air mixture into the cylinder past the open inlet valve.

(2) *Compression.* When the piston has completed its down-stroke, the inlet valve closes. The revolving crankshaft then pushes the piston up again, and the mixture now in the cylinder is compressed upward into the combustion chamber. At the top of the stroke it is fully compressed.

(3) *Ignition* (Firing). At this point a spark occurs between the electrodes of the sparking plug. This ignites the petrol/air mixture. The heat from the explosion causes high pressure on the top of the piston which is thus forced downward.

(4) *Exhaust.* At the end of this down-stroke, the exhaust valve opens and during the following up-stroke the products of combustion are pushed past the valve and out of the engine. This cycle is constantly repeated so long as the engine is running.

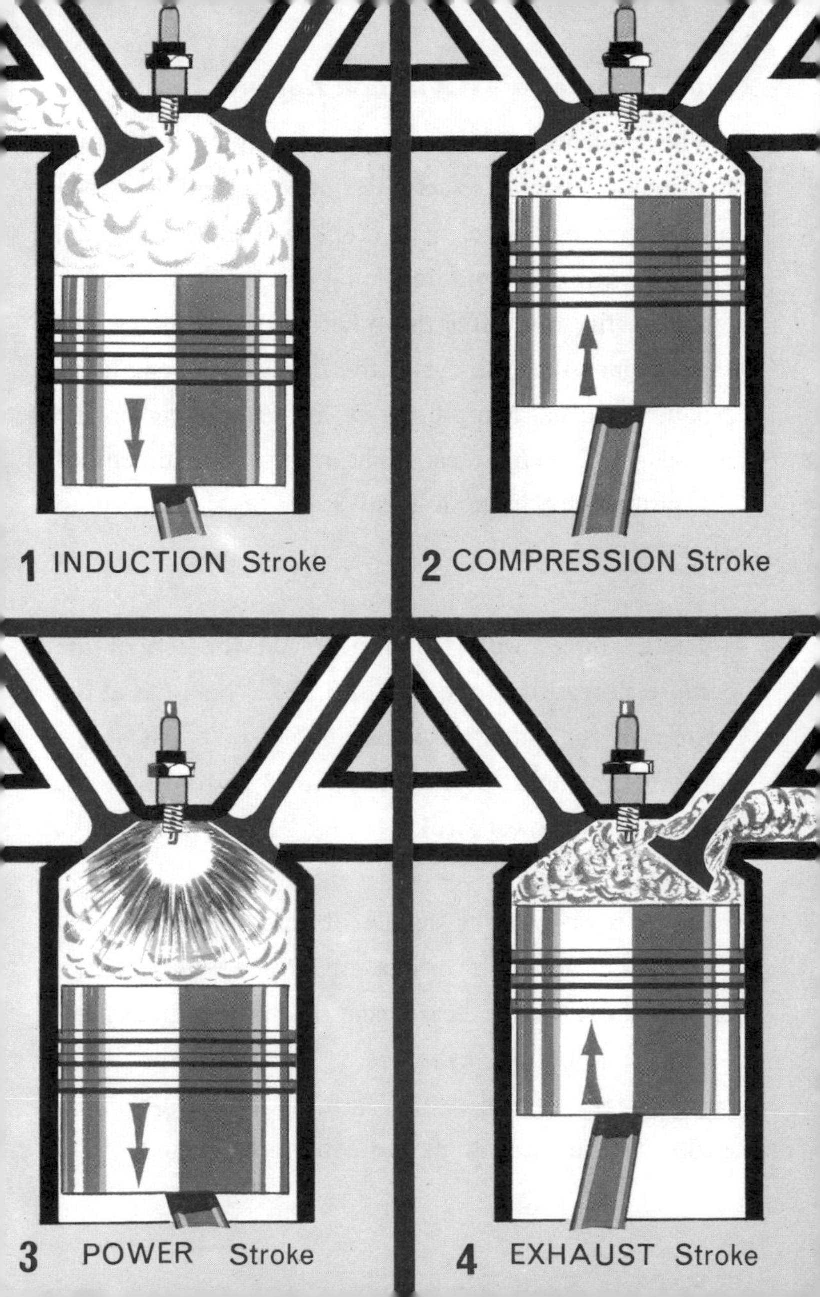
1 INDUCTION Stroke
2 COMPRESSION Stroke
3 POWER Stroke
4 EXHAUST Stroke

### *Operation of a 4-Cylinder Engine*

The sequence of operation for an engine with more than one cylinder is exactly the same as that described on the previous page. The crankshaft is so designed, and the valve and ignition timing so arranged, that the cylinders fire one after the other in quick succession. If we regard the cylinder at the front of the engine as No. 1, the usual firing order of a four-cylinder engine is 1 - 3 - 4 - 2. This means that at any one moment all the pistons are in a different stage of the operating sequence.

For example: with No. 1 piston at the top of the compression stroke (about to fire), No. 3 piston is at the bottom of the induction stroke, No. 4 piston is at the top of the exhaust stroke, and No. 2 piston is at the bottom of the power stroke.

In a single-cylinder engine of the type commonly used on a motor-cycle, or in a small three-wheeler car, a distinct 'beat' can be heard each time the cylinder fires. As the number of cylinders is increased the 'beat' becomes less definite so that in a six- or eight-cylinder engine it is heard as an almost continuous sound.

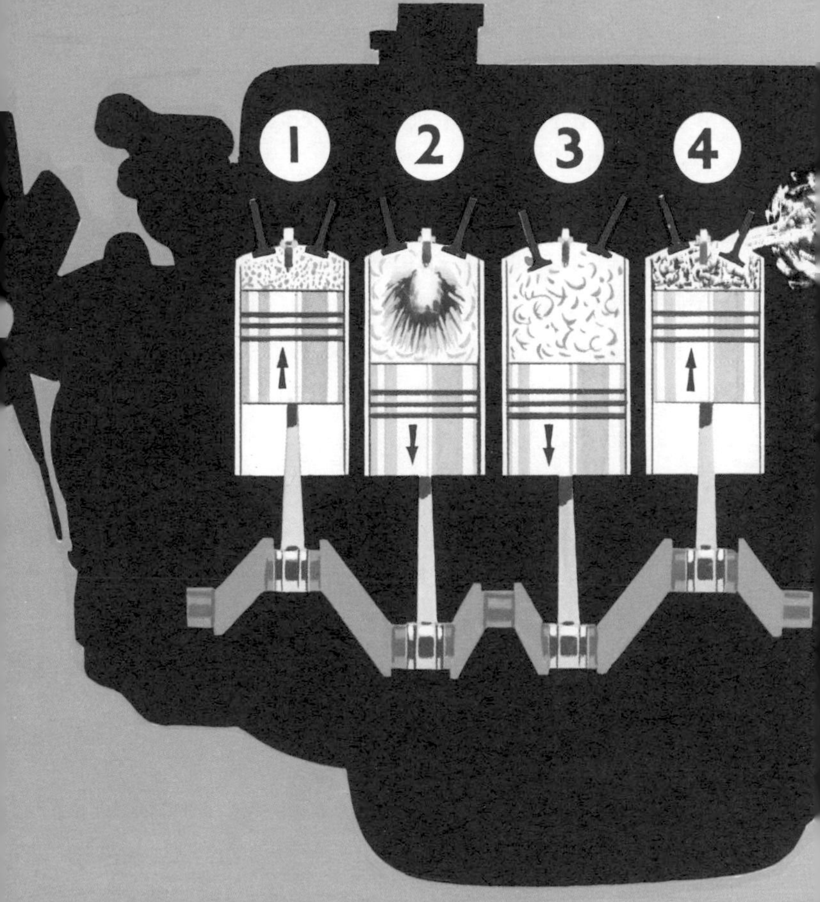
1
2
3
4

## *The Cooling System*

Engines become very hot while they are running, due to the intense heat created by combustion. Some form of cooling must therefore be adopted and in most cars water is used.

The water enters the cylinder block near the bottom of the cylinders, and flows through special passages cast in the cylinder block and cylinder head. As it absorbs the engine heat its temperature increases and this causes it to flow upward. When it reaches the top of the engine the water is very hot. Now the water itself must be cooled, otherwise it would boil. This is done by means of a radiator. The hot water leaves the top of the engine and filters through the radiator where it is cooled by the passage of air. As it cools it falls to the bottom of the radiator from where it re-enters the engine.

In older engines water circulated in this way without assistance (*known as thermo-syphon circulation*), but its movement was rather slow and the cooling effect was limited. In modern engines a pump, driven by the fan belt, helps to force the water through the system and so improves its cooling efficiency.

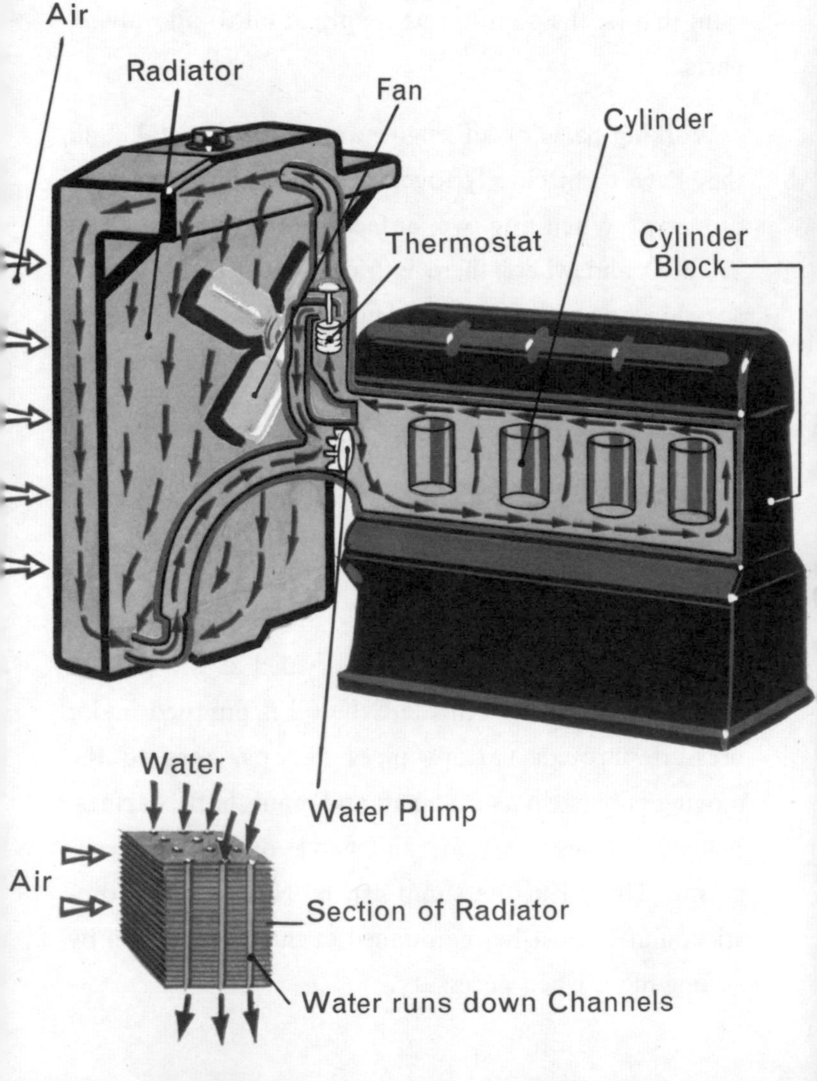
Air
Radiator
Fan
Cylinder
Thermostat
Cylinder Block
Water
Water Pump
Air
Section of Radiator
Water runs down Channels

## *Engine Lubrication*

Another essential requirement of an engine is lubrication, that is, the continuous supply of oil to all moving parts.

Working parts of an engine are made of metal, and they have to fit closely together if they are to function properly. When any two surfaces rub together there is 'friction' and where there is friction heat is produced. In cold weather we rub our hands together to keep them warm, and it is the friction between the surface of one hand and the other that produces the desired warmth. In an engine this extra heat must be avoided or the parts will wear out quickly and become damaged. Oil greatly reduces friction and allows the parts to run smoothly together.

An oil reservoir, *or sump*, is provided at the bottom of the engine, and from there the oil is pumped under pressure through various pipes and passages to the moving parts such as camshaft and crankshaft bearings, big-end bearings, pistons and valve operating mechanism. The oil in the sump can be checked by a dipstick, and it must be maintained at the correct level by adding more when necessary.

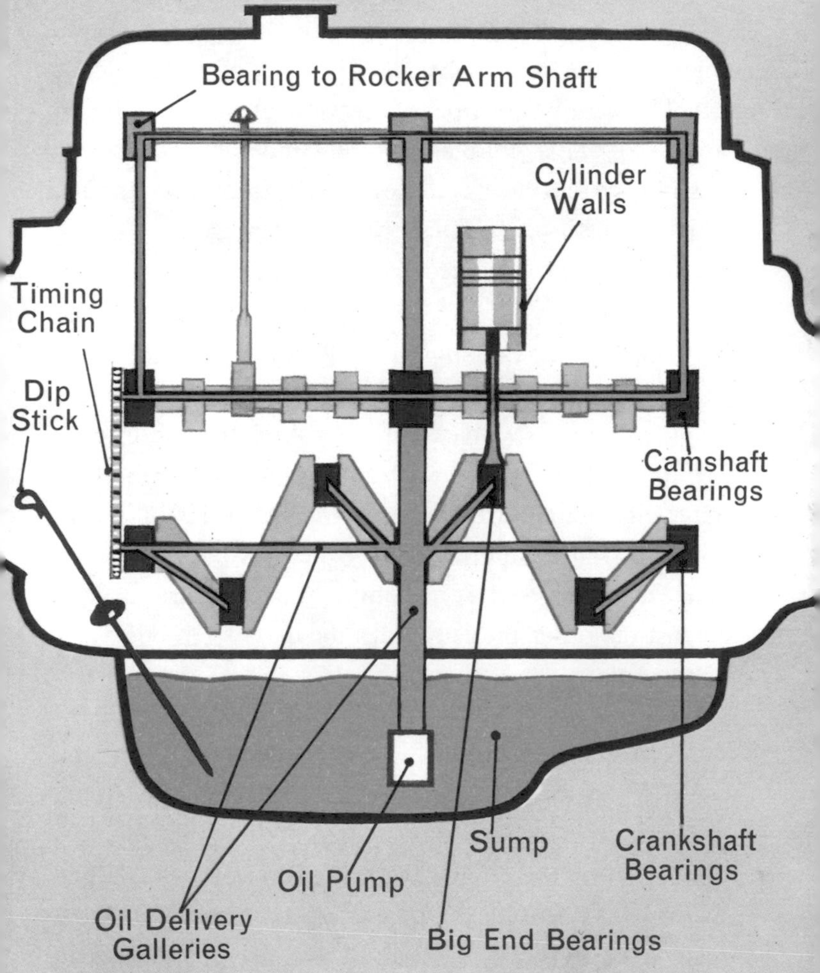
Bearing to Rocker Arm Shaft
Cylinder Walls
Timing Chain
Dip Stick
Camshaft Bearings
Sump
Crankshaft Bearings
Oil Pump
Oil Delivery Galleries
Big End Bearings

## *The Clutch*

The transmission system of a car is a series of assemblies whose purpose is to transmit the power of the engine to the road wheels. The first of these is the *clutch* assembly, an opened-up view of which is shown opposite. This enables the remainder of the transmission system to be disconnected from the engine, when necessary, so that the various gears in the gearbox can be engaged (*see page 33*).

At the back of the engine is a heavy flat wheel known as the flywheel. It is attached to the rear end of the crankshaft and revolves with it. A clutch plate, consisting of a metal disc with a friction lining round its outer edge, is held firmly against the flywheel by a spring-loaded pressure plate. As the flywheel revolves the clutch plate revolves, and it is simply the pressure of one against the other that provides the drive from engine to transmission.

The clutch is operated by the clutch pedal inside the car. When the driver depresses the pedal the clutch pressure plate is forced away from the flywheel, thus disconnecting the engine from the transmission. When the pedal is released, the pressure plate forces the clutch plate against the flywheel and the drive is taken up again.

Flywheel
Cover
Pedal Linkage
Clutch Centre Plate
Pressure Plate

Clutch Out
Clutch in

## *The Gearbox*

The object of the *gearbox* is to provide a means of obtaining the most efficient engine speed in relation to the speed required at the road wheels.

The gearbox is quite a complicated assembly of gears of different sizes, arranged so that certain combinations of gears can be engaged to enable one to drive another. If a larger gear drives a smaller one, a high ratio is produced, and if a smaller gear drives a larger one a lower ratio is provided. Most car gearboxes have four 'speeds', which means that by moving the gear lever inside the car one of four different ratios can be selected in the gearbox. A reverse gear is also included to enable the car to be driven backwards for manœuvring.

To illustrate the gearbox principle in a simple manner, the arrangement of gears in a three-speed box only are shown.

In a low ratio gear the engine runs fast while the car is moving quite slowly. As higher gears are engaged the engine speed drops but the car moves faster. A low ratio is therefore used when greater engine power is needed to start the car from rest, to accelerate quickly and to climb steep hills. For normal cruising along a road, a high gear is selected.

Top Gear

Second Gear

Bottom Gear

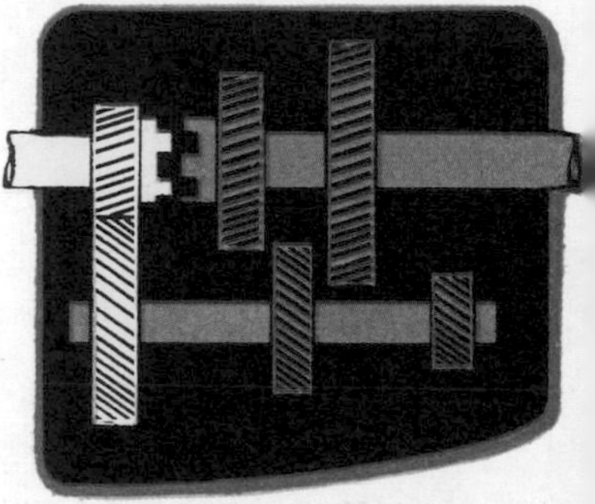

Neutral

Gears in use

Gears not in use

Reverse Gear

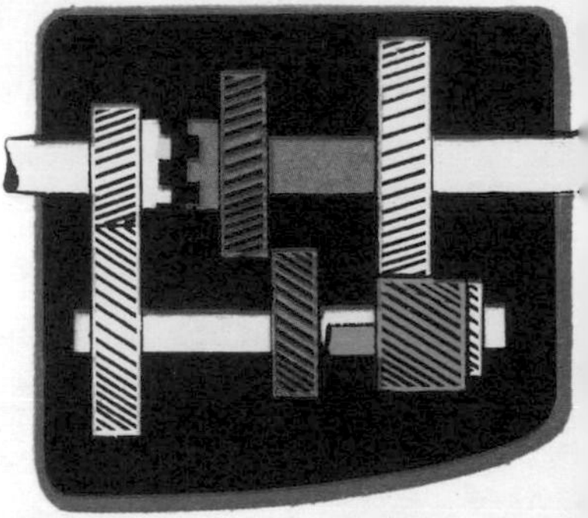

Reverse

In Gear

### *Overdrive*

*Overdrive units* are now available on a great many cars, either as a standard fitting or as an extra to be fitted if required. The purpose of an overdrive is to provide an additional gear of higher ratio than is available in the normal gearbox. The unit is fitted behind the gearbox, but is entirely independent and not affected by movements of the ordinary gear lever. The usual control for the overdrive is a small lever or switch. When the switch is flicked to 'on', electrical contact is made and the special gear in the overdrive takes over. When the switch is flicked off normal drive is resumed.

There are several advantages in having this extra overdrive gear. Because the ratio is high the speed of the engine is slower for any given road wheel speed, this means that the engine runs more smoothly, consumes less petrol and there is less wear of the parts. Another important advantage is a marked reduction in mechanical noise and vibration.

Various overdrive systems are in use. In some types, engagement is only possible when top gear of the normal gearbox is engaged. In other types overdrive can also be selected in one or more of the lower gears, thus giving a greater number of intermediate gears.

Overdrive
Switch

Overdrive
behind Gearbox

## *Automatic Transmission*

While many drivers like to control their cars by the normal gearbox and gear change lever, some motorists prefer to drive with as little effort as possible. That is why a *fully automatic transmission* is sometimes made available, but because of its size it is usually supplied only for larger cars. This system takes much of the work away from the driver, who merely has to accelerate when he wants to go faster and brake when he wishes to slow down or stop. All the necessary gear changing is done quite automatically within the transmission. There is no gear lever and no clutch pedal, only a selector arm.

The automatic transmission is fitted in place of the normal gearbox and clutch unit. A control lever near the steering wheel has five positions: P (*park*), N (*neutral*), D (*drive*), L (*low*), R (*reverse*).

In position 'P' the transmission is locked and the car cannot be moved. At 'N' the engine can be started but the transmission is not engaged. All normal driving is done with the lever at 'D'. 'L' is a special low gear position for starting on a steep slope, climbing steep hills, or for holding low gear whilst accelerating.

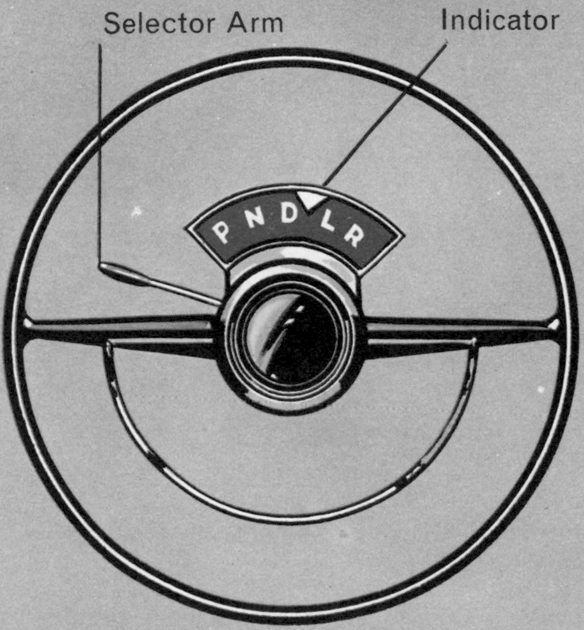


No Clutch Pedal

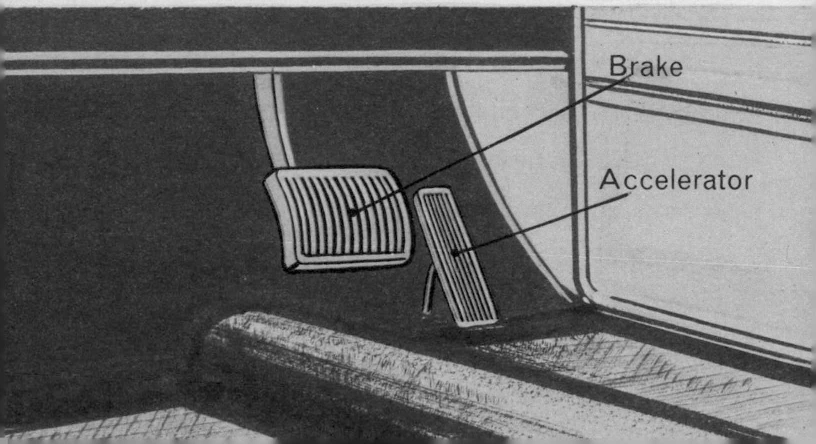

### *The Rear Axle*

The *rear axle* is the final unit in the transmission system, and it is connected to the gearbox by a long tube known as the *propeller shaft*. The rear axle has four jobs to do: (1) It carries the rear road wheels. (2) It transmits the drive to the wheels. (3) It reduces the ratio of the drive from the gearbox and turns it through a right-angle. That is to say, it converts the right to left rotation of the propeller shaft into the forward or backward rotation of the road wheels. (4) It allows for 'differential action' (*see page 40*).

The rear axle drive consists of a small toothed wheel known as the 'pinion', which is joined to the propeller shaft, and a large toothed wheel (the 'crown wheel'), which is driven by the pinion. The difference between the number of crown wheel and pinion teeth gives the rear axle ratio. For instance, if the crown wheel has 48 teeth and the pinion has 12, the ratio is 48 to 12, or 4 to 1. A high ratio gives a faster top speed with slower acceleration, while a low ratio gives a slower top speed but faster acceleration. The car designer must balance the two to give a good all-round performance.

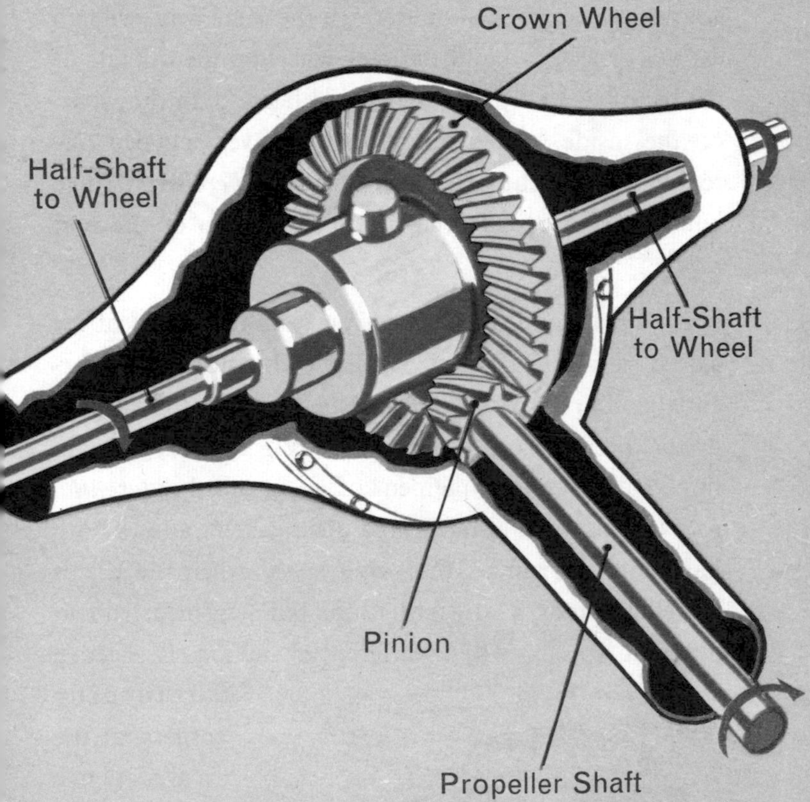
Crown Wheel
Half-Shaft to Wheel
Half-Shaft to Wheel
Pinion
Propeller Shaft

### *The Rear Axle Differential Action*

If you extend your arm to one side, then swing it round to the front of your body, the tips of your fingers have to travel further and faster than the part of your arm near your shoulder. In the same way, when a car goes round a bend the rear wheel on the outside of the bend has to travel further and faster than the wheel on the inside. This difference of travel between one rear wheel and the other is known as *differential action*, and it has to be allowed for in the design of the rear axle.

Each rear road wheel is driven from the centre of the axle by a half-shaft, but because of the need for differential action the inner ends of the half-shafts cannot be driven directly from the crown wheel. Instead, they are fitted within an arrangement of gears called *differential gears*. This quite complicated arrangement allows both half-shafts to run at the same speed when the car is travelling along a straight road, but lets them run at different speeds when differential action is needed for turning corners, at the same time keeping power on each driving wheel.

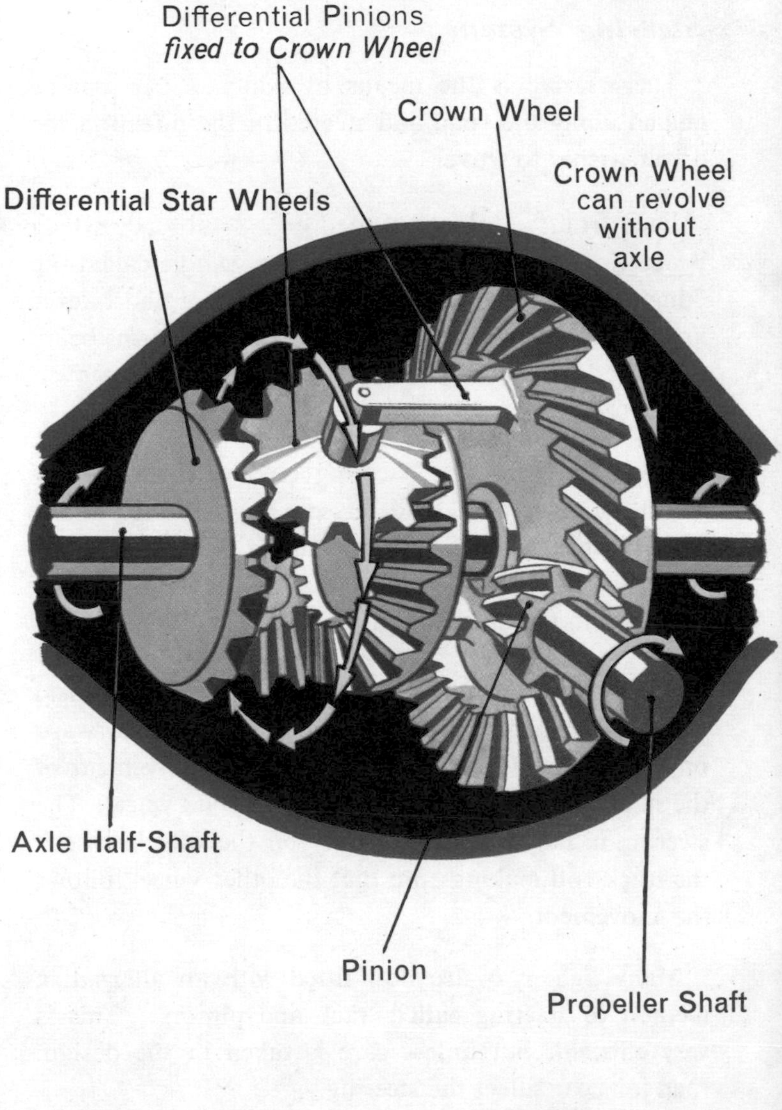

Differential Pinions
*fixed to Crown Wheel*
Crown Wheel
Crown Wheel can revolve without axle
Differential Star Wheels
Axle Half-Shaft
Pinion
Propeller Shaft

### *Steering System*

The *steering* is the means by which a car can be guided along the road and steered in the direction the driver wishes to travel.

Each front wheel is mounted on a 'stub' axle which is able to swivel on a nearly upright spindle called the 'king-pin'. Fitted to each stub axle is a short lever known as the 'steering arm', the two steering arms being connected together across the front of the car by a 'track-rod'.

Projecting from the 'steering box' is a short lever called the 'drop arm', and this can be connected to the off-side wheel (the wheel on the driver's side of the car) by means of a 'drag-link', or directly to the track rod as shown in the illustration.

When the driver turns the steering wheel, mechanism in the steering box causes the drop arm to move forward or backward. This movement results in movement of the steering arm and the turning of the road wheel. The steering usually operates directly on the offside wheel, the track rod making sure that the other wheel follows the movement.

Many light cars are now fitted with an alternative method of steering called 'rack and pinion'. This is very efficient, but unless care is taken in the design, road jolts can affect the steering.

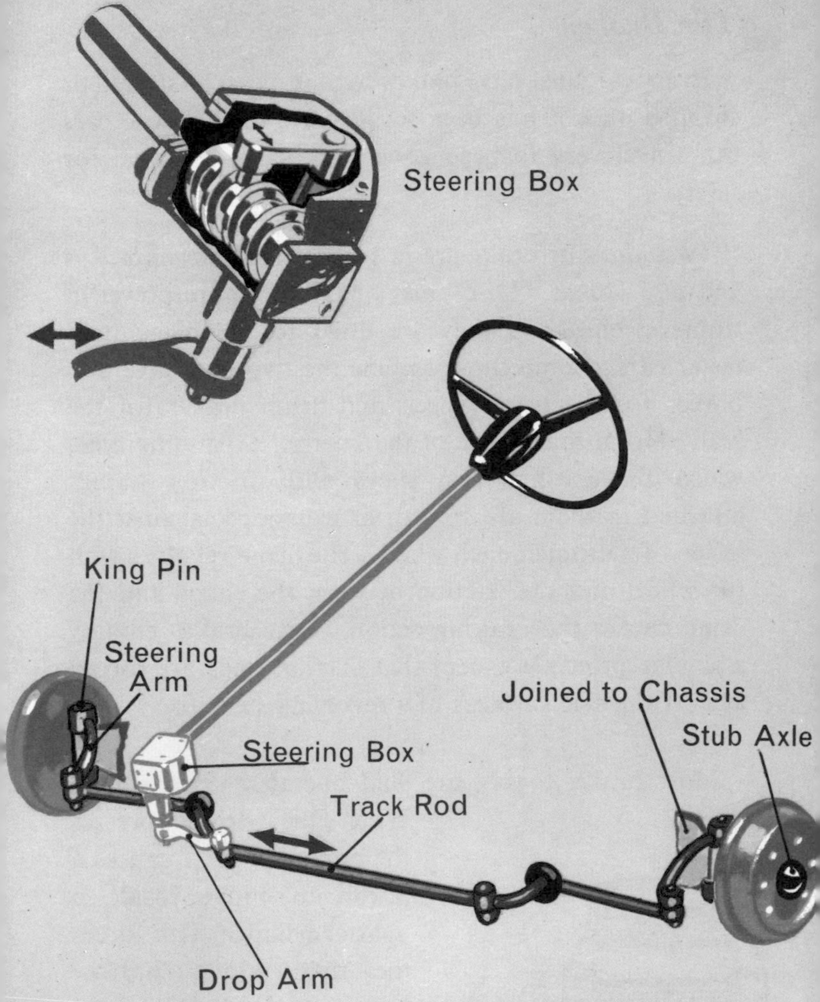
Steering Box
King Pin
Steering
Arm
Joined to Chassis
Stub Axle
Steering Box
Track Rod
Drop Arm

### *The Brakes*

Every car must have brakes so that it can be slowed or stopped once it has been set in motion. Modern cars can travel very fast, so good brakes are essential for safety.

Two kinds of brake are in general use: *Drum brakes* and *disc brakes.* Disc brakes have the more powerful stopping effect, so they are fitted to the bigger and faster cars. Some cars combine the two and have disc brakes for the front wheels and drum brakes for the rear. Drum brakes are of the internal expanding type, which means that two shoes with friction linings attached to them are forced, or expanded, against the inside of a drum at each wheel. The drum revolves with the wheel and the friction between the shoes and the drum causes the braking action. Disc brakes employ a similar principle except that friction pads are forced against the side surfaces of a revolving steel disc.

Most brakes to-day arc fluid operated ('hydraulic'). When the driver presses the brake pedal, it causes a piston to move inside a 'master cylinder'. This forces the fluid along narrow pipes to each wheel where a small piston is pushed outward to operate the shoes.

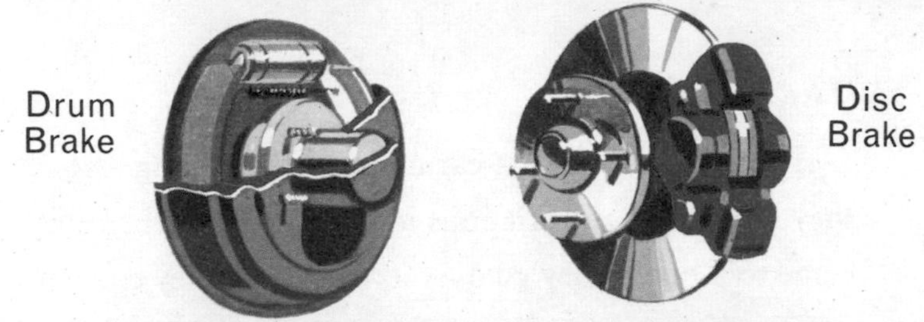
Drum
Brake
Disc
Brake

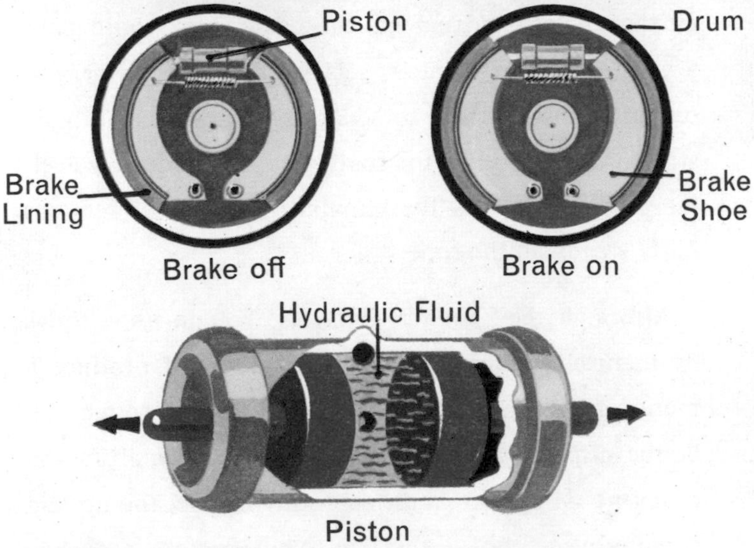
Piston
Drum
Brake
Lining
Brake
Shoe
Brake off
Brake on
Hydraulic Fluid
Piston

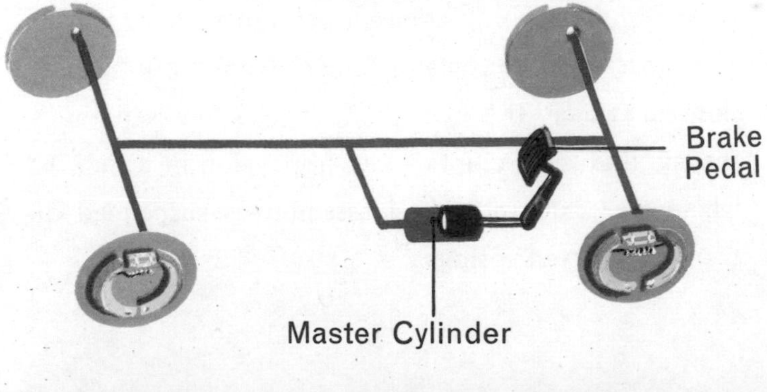
Brake
Pedal
Master Cylinder

## *The Suspension*

When the wheels of a car are travelling along a road they follow all the variations in the surface. When they come to a bump they go over it, and when they come to a hollow they go into it. If the whole car had to follow all these wheel movements the passengers would have a very jerky ride. The wheels are therefore suspended on springs which help to separate them from the body structure, and even if the road is bumpy and the wheels jump up and down, the remainder of the car remains fairly steady all the time.

Although they smooth out road roughness, springs by themselves have too much bounce and produce a motion rather like that of a small boat on a rough sea. So the *suspension system* has to include shock absorbers or spring dampers. These smoothly restrict the up and down movement of the springs to give a more level ride.

There are many different suspension systems in use. The most usual consists of 'independent front suspension' in which the two front wheels are separately sprung, and 'semi-elliptic' rear suspension in which the whole rear axle and wheel assembly is suspended on two long, curved springs.

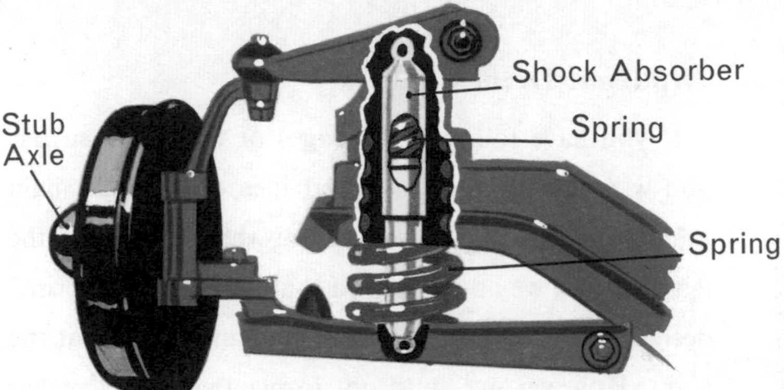

Front Suspension

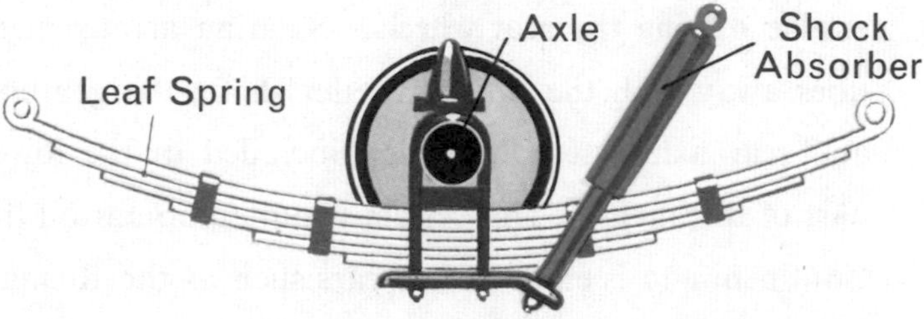

Rear Suspension

Top line shows Body Movement
Bottom line shows Wheel Movement

### *Different Drives*

If you have followed the pages of this book so far, you will now have a very good idea of how the main units of a motor car work. For the purpose of the descriptions, we have assumed that our car is of normal design with a front-mounted engine and an axle at the rear. However, we must not forget that many makes of cars are designed differently.

The most common variation is a rear-mounted engine driving the rear wheels. Such an arrangement does away with the long propeller shaft; the gearbox and rear axle assemblies being included in the lower part of the engine. This system is quite popular on the Continent and is employed on cars such as the Renault Dauphine and Volkswagen. In Britain the Hillman Imp is the only mass-produced car to have a rear engine, at the time of writing.

Another arrangement is to have a front-mounted engine driving the front wheels. The B.M.C. Minis are a good example of this, but they have the added difference of an engine mounted sideways across the car instead of the usual forward and backward fitting.

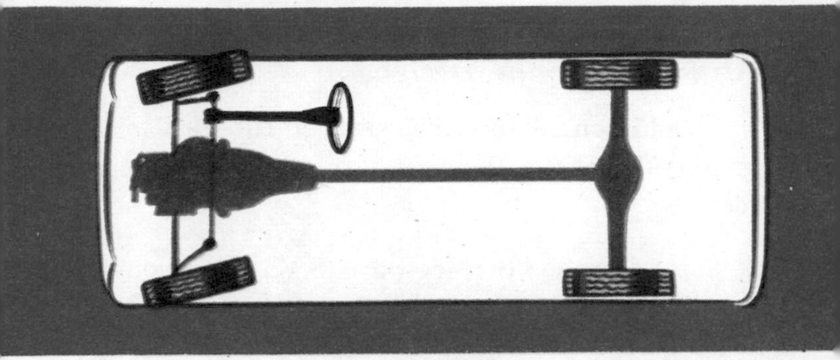

Conventional Drive

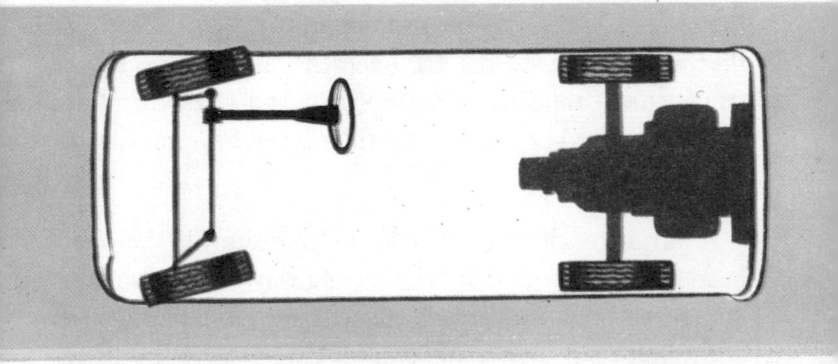

Rear Engine Drive

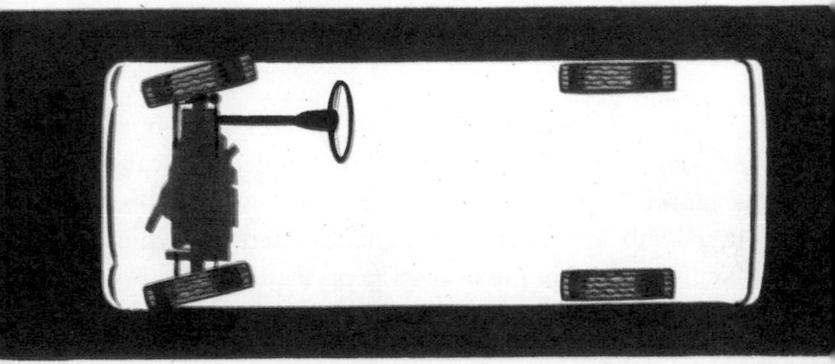

Front Engine Drive

### *Different Engine Designs*

In addition to the different methods available for driving the wheels, there are also many different engine designs.

Some years ago the side-valve (S.V.) engine was very popular. In this not-very-efficient design the valves were placed at the side of the cylinders. The great majority of modern engines are of the overhead-valve type (o.h.v.) in which the valves are positioned above the pistons with their heads facing downward. Because the valve stems, in this arrangement, are some distance from the camshaft, 'push-rods' and 'rockers' are normally used to provide the necessary means of operation.

A variation of the overhead-valve design is the overhead camshaft (o.h.c.). This does away with push-rods and sometimes rockers, because the camshaft is fitted above the valve stems and can operate directly on them.

Some engines combine the overhead- and side-valve systems and have overhead inlet valves and side exhaust valves.

There are also the V-type and 'horizontally-opposed' engines, and others. The whole subject of cars and engines is a fascinating one. Now you know more about it you will be able to take a greater interest in your own family car and in those you see on the roads.